W9-CMV-073

A WORD TO PARENTS AND TEACHERS

Jesus started us all thinking about Christian missions. He said, "Go ye . . . " to our home town, the lands around, and the lands across the sea. The Christian missionary movement is as old as the visit of the Baby Jesus to the manger, an ambassador of love from a faraway place. This book seeks to build early thoughts about missions in the mind of your child. It helps him to think of others who need to know about Jesus—and what they need to know. It talks of children around the world, and those in our own back yard. And it shows how the Gospel of Christ is delightfully at home in jungles, frozen lands of the Eskimos, the islands of the sea, or anywhere. AROUND THE WORLD WITH MY RED BALLOON combines many important truths about Jesus Christ with this missionary emphasis and brings it all to your child in a story about a big red balloon. Balloons of this size are used today for weather research and may even be purchased by private citizens who want to dream of going AROUND THE WORLD IN THEIR RED BALLOON.

Printed in the United States of America

AROUND THE WORLD WITH MY RED BALLOON

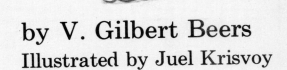

by V. Gilbert Beers

Illustrated by Juel Krisvoy

THE SOUTHWESTERN COMPANY

Nashville, Tennessee

©1973 by V. Gilbert Beers

If I could go
with my red balloon
to places far away,
I'd soar above
the highest clouds
and float across
the widest seas.

I'd go to lands
around the world—
around the world
with my red balloon.

If I could take
my very best friend,
and we could go
where we've never been,
we'd visit children
around the world—
around the world
with my red balloon.

If we could go
to Eskimo lands,
where children live
in round igloos,
and dress in parkas
made of fur,
we'd play with them
upon the snow

and ride in long sleds
pulled by dogs,
or fish through holes
cut in the ice.
We'd watch the seal
and walrus play
with polar bears
near Arctic seas.

We'd tell that Jesus
is God's Son,
and how He left
His home in heaven,
and came to earth
to show the way
that we must take
to get to God.

If we could go
to Africa,
where long grass waves
near jungle streams,
where zebras play
with tall giraffes,
and lions live
with elephants,
we'd hear the chants
of witch doctors,
and know their way
is very bad.

We'd play with children
in the shade
of jungle trees
with wide green leaves,
and go with them
inside their huts
with walls of mud
and roofs of grass.

And then we'd tell
how Jesus came
to die upon
a cross for us,
to take away
the sin we have,
and show us how
to follow Him.

If we could go
around the world,
with my red balloon
to the Orient,
we'd sit beneath
a parasol

and eat some rice
with wood chopsticks,
or watch the fishing
boats sail by,
where Buddha's temples
touch the sky.

We'd tell our friends
that Jesus lives—
how He came back
to life again.
And how He rose
up in the sky
to go back home
to live in heaven.

If we could go
around the world—
around the world
with my red balloon,
we'd go away
to magic lands,
the tropic islands
of the sea.

We'd play with friends
by coconut palms,
and gather seashells
on the beach.

We'd swim across
a coral reef
or paddle in
a strange canoe.
We'd hear some tell
of their strange gods,
which no one loves,
but all men fear.

And underneath
a banana tree,
we'd tell how Jesus
loves us so,
and how He goes
with us each day
when we choose Him
as our best Friend.

If we could go
with my red balloon
to South America,
we'd sing with friends
who play guitars
and wear sombreros
on their heads.
We'd laugh as parrots
fly above
and monkeys play
among the trees.

We'd tell our friends,
"The Bible says
what Jesus did,
and what He said."
We'd ask if they
would think and pray,
and give their lives
to follow Him.

But we'd come home
with my red balloon,
and stop awhile
in my back yard.
We'd watch our friends
come running there
to hear about
the things we'd done.

And then we'd tell
what we had said
to other friends
around the world.
We'd tell how Jesus
loves them, too,
and wants them each
to follow Him.

And when we thought
of all we'd done,
we'd bow our heads
and thank God, too,
for going with us
everywhere—
around the world
with my red balloon.